Collected S

Also by Ann Lax and published by Ginninderra Press
Collected Poems

Ann Lax

Collected Stories

Collected Stories
ISBN 978 1 76109 374 6
Copyright © text Ann Lax 2022

First published 2022 by
GINNINDERRA PRESS
PO Box 3461 Port Adelaide 5015
www.ginninderrapress.com.au

Contents

The Trap

My cousins, Rod and Harvey Pratt breezed in on a cloud of expensive cologne, dressed in black Versace suits (probably bought for the funeral), pointed Italian shoes and silk ties.

'Under the circumstances, I didn't expect to see you here, cousin.' Rod looked down his nose at me.

I shrugged with what I hoped was disdain. 'I've as much right to be here as you, Rod.'

Mister Peabody, our uncle's solicitor, had directed us to be present at the reading of his will. It was there that I first became aware of my uncle's taste for intrigue.

'I rather thought you'd blotted your copybook, Chris.'

Rod's smirk sent chills down my spine. I hoped the solicitor wasn't listening. I was eyeball to eyeball with him and, given the state of my conscience, I focused on his bobbing Adam's apple instead. I squirmed, straightened my wool tie and kept my feet flat on the ground in case my soles were worn.

'Money would be wasted on you. You've got no style,' laughed Harvey.

With glossy black hair and flint eyes, my cousins sat bolt upright in their chairs. If I'd inherited the wrong genes, at least I hadn't inherited those steely eyes. My mother and I were poor relations from the poorer end of town. Their family passed on used clothes, old toys and, most humiliating of all. uneaten food.

I smoothed my hair over my balding pate. My thoughts focused on the shiny seat of my suit pants and the rubbed elbows of my coat, and I began to finger the rash under my collar.

The perpetrator of my uncle's hit and run accident hadn't been found and the police didn't have any leads. It cast a pall over what was already a solemn event.

The solicitor cleared his throat. His voice was sardonic and gruff as he finally began discussing the will.

'The terms of the will are rather unusual and before your uncle's estate can be disbursed, you have been set a task. Your uncle, as you know, valued initiative…'

My uncle had called me to his office just after the HSC. 'Chris, I have high hopes for you. Keep on in this vein and I will support you through university and after.'

I felt a rush of satisfaction. My hard work had paid off.

Then followed one of his long and morose silences. I shuffled my feet and wondered if I'd inherited his tendency to depression. He went on, 'But you may have inherited your father's weaknesses. Take care.'

My father died just after I was born so I never knew him.

In a dismissive tone, he brought up the subject of my cousins. 'If Rod and Harvey want to get on in this world, they'll have to learn it's not just about appearances.' He added as I got up to leave, 'You should realise with your abilities you attract jealousy.'

He was the one person whose advice I could trust, so I took it to heart. His watery blue eyes bored into mine and I realised he knew more that he was letting on.

I straightened in my chair and glanced at my cousins. They didn't look in my direction. Were they suffering pangs of conscience? Not likely.

The room was crammed with law books in floor-to-ceiling oak bookcases and I began to feel oppressed. It reminded me that if my firm had brought the full weight of the law to bear, I would have been jailed for embezzlement. As it was, I had been let off with a caution not to work in accountancy again.

That Monday morning when I was summoned to the boss's office was something I'd never forget.

My boss demanded, 'You know why I've summoned you here today?'

They knew what I'd done so I saw no reason to stall.

'I've been embezzling the company for two years.'

'Who else was involved?'

'It was my own initiative. I deeply regret my actions.'

'Did your friends have any knowledge of this?'

'I told no one.'

'Were drugs or alcohol an issue?'

'No, sir.'

I found out much later it was my uncle's good word for me that had saved me from incarceration.

I'm surprised that I'm here today. My uncle was a stickler for honesty. I had gone to counselling for six months to overcome my gambling addiction and I avoid the gambling websites on the Internet. When I began the session, my uncle revealed that my father was a gambler. The counsellor said my addiction was hereditary.

I'd valued the good opinion of my uncle very highly. We'd never been close but after my father died he'd been like a bulwark in the background until this.

'Mister Duffy,' the solicitor called my name sharply and gave me a withering look. 'This concerns you as well as your cousins. I will have to repeat myself. Your uncle has left instructions that the will has been hidden in the house. You have been given a day to locate its hiding place and then return here with it by five p.m. to await further directions.'

Rod's jaw had dropped, exposing his back molars, and Harvey had turned pale under his sunlamp tan. This wasn't the first time I'd found myself in competition with my cousins. We were the same age and in the same year at high school. They excelled at athletics; with my clumsy body, I was inept. They'd be at the finishing line ages before me and urge me on with a faintly jeering tone.

I spent many lunch hours in the library to avoid them and their jibes. They were very popular, while I hung out with the nerds. Praise in the classroom didn't make for popularity in the schoolyard. My cousins introduced me to gambling. They organised two-up games in the lunch hour and I was a willing participant. Partly for the camaraderie and partly for the highs when I won.

I was astonished at the ease with which they could manipulate their friends. They paid more gifted schoolmates to produce projects and assignments they handed in as their own work. I still can't believe how they got away with it.

I confronted Rod about it on one memorable occasion, which was difficult for me as I disliked showdowns. He was with several of the mates who'd been useful to him.

'What you're doing is dishonest and doesn't help you in the long run.'

Rod's lip curled in a sneer. 'Are you going to dob, little cousin?'

His friends looked alarmed and one clenched his fists as though he'd like to punch me.

'Your life won't be worth living if you do,' he muttered.

Of course I backed down and slunk off.

The inevitable was they flunked final exams. The highlight of my year was speech night. I received several prizes. But best of all I wouldn't have to see the terrible twosome for a couple of months.

I saw Rod and Harvey scuttle into the hallway of my uncle's two-storey Georgian house as I walked from the bus stop. I climbed the steps to the porch and rang the bell. There was no answer. I tried again and again. My uncle's housekeeper, Ellen, must have let them in and had instructions to admit me too. Although I had visited my uncle many times, she seemed to dislike me.

I pressed the buzzer so hard it jammed and finally Ellen opened the door grumbling. The musty smell of the hallway mingled with the cloying scent of roses. She'd been arranging a bouquet of roses next to the lavish heart-shaped box of chocolates on the hall stand. I guessed they were gifts from my cousins.

I fingered my last fifty dollars in my pocket. On my way over, I'd tried to give it to a homeless man but after looking me up and down he'd brushed it aside and said, 'You look down on your luck too, mate. I can't take it.'

'Where are they, Ellen?'

'Upstairs,' she said. She jerked her thumb over her bony shoulder and turned away.

I wondered if she and her peevishness were part of the inheritance. This was not a pleasant thought. Ellen had been with my uncle for forty years and he would not have left her unprovided for. She muttered something about making herself a cup of coffee and wandered off.

I could hear from upstairs the sound of filing cabinet drawers being opened and slammed shut in my uncle's office. My cousins glanced up as I entered the doorway.

'Missed the boat as always, Chris,' smirked Rod.

'You're very sure of yourself,' I countered.

'You'd do yourself a favour if you'd just walk away. You're in the big league here.'

His attitude aroused my suspicions. They must have hatched something between them. Papers had been tossed everywhere and the room was a shambles. I bent down to retrieve some and was sent sprawling to the floor with a shove in the back. Before I could recover, I heard the door slam and a key turn in the lock.

'See if you can escape from there, little cousin.'

There wasn't much hope that I would get out. My uncle was very security conscious. The door was deadlocked and of solid wood. I would have to sit it out. There was no phone in the room so I couldn't ring out. I rubbed the rabbit's foot in my pocket. I spent my time searching the office but there was no sign of a will.

After several hours of their rummaging downstairs, the house fell silent. I'd call out to Ellen repeatedly but there was no reply. At a quarter to five, bored and indifferent, she unlocked the door.

It was almost dusk when I left my uncle's street. I arrived back at the solicitor's ten minutes late and with a feeling of humiliation. My cousins had outwitted me again. The solicitor was drumming his fingers on the desk and peered over the top of his glasses at me as I slid into my chair. My cousins oozed smugness.

'Now that we're all here, we can begin.'

I squirmed.

'Rod and Harvey have produced a will. This seems to show the initiative valued by your uncle but unfortunately they have been too clever. Their will has been forged. The original will has been here all along, so it puts a question mark over the lengths to which they will go to gain their ends. This was a task to see how you all would act under particular circumstances. Your uncle knew of your brush with the law, Mr Duffy, and also of your relationship with your cousins. Despite your past and since this exercise showed you didn't take the opportunity to act fraudulently, Mr Duffy, you will have control of your share. Rod and Harvey's share will be put in trust.'

The drone of the solicitor's voice was interrupted by the shrill ring of the telephone at his elbow. I'd been so absorbed in what he was saying that I jumped in my chair.

The solicitor hung up after a brief call. He looked over the top of his glasses at my cousins and me. 'That was the police. They are coming tomorrow to ask further questions regarding your uncle's death.' He resumed the reading. 'The cousins will only get the interest on the principal and I will be in control. If misfortune befalls any one of you, their inheritance will revert to the other parties. Provided there are no suspicious circumstances involved in such misfortune. There is the matter of your uncle's housekeeper. As Rod and Harvey have always taken a keen interest in her, they are to take charge of her welfare. Their access to their portion depends on their carrying this out satisfactorily. Your uncle's accident is still under investigation. The police apparently have several leads now.'

The windfall would certainly solve all my problems. It was all I could do to control my excitement. But there was the business of the accident. As beneficiaries of the will, were we being scrutinised? Were Rod and Harvey involved in the hit and run? I knew they were money-hungry and capable of anything. My share was considerable. Would they have their eyes on that?

Harvey was robbing his index finger back and forth along his lower lip and the speculation in his eyes as he focused on me sent twinges of fear creeping up and down my spine.

There Are More Things

I remember when our neighbour Elvira Brown moved in and hammered a sign on her front gate, 'Herbalist – Tarot readings by appointment'.

'Hi!' she called from over the fence shortly after but Dad ignored her and went on hosing his camellias.

He fussed and fidgeted. 'One of those New Age types. Mark my words, she'll be trouble.'

I wish this had been one of Dad's usual pie-in-the-sky prophecies, but things did start to go awry. He was preparing for our local garden competition and was afraid she didn't look like a gardener. Her untidy yard could blight his chances and competition was very fierce.

Once Dad saw the headlines of our local rag, 'Six Garden Gnomes Stolen. Police Investigating,' his blue eyes bulged. 'I hope this is not the beginning of an assault on gardens, Jake. Personally I think garden gnomes are tacky but some of the competitors indulge in statuary of various kinds. I wouldn't like to think they were unfairly targeted.' Dad wasn't the slightest bit concerned about anyone else but the news made him nervous.

Our previous neighbour had been elderly and had let her garden go to rack and ruin. Those were Dad's words. This was really just a matter of a growth of canes overhanging Dad's pride and joy – his topiary in the shape of a bird.

Since my mother had run away with the piano tuner, Dad had had very little to do with females. So the job of asking Elvira Brown to kindly prune her shrub fell to me. The normal step would have been to cut the offending items himself. But it was Dad's way to make mountains out of molehills.

At thirteen going on fourteen, this prospect didn't daunt me at all. I had long been interested in magic and with her skills (and didn't her black cat Mabel never leave her side?) perhaps she could give me some pointers.

I always knew when she was in the yard because I could hear the jingle of her bracelets. Taking a deep breath, I sauntered over to the fence. 'Ahem,' I ventured.

She looked around and stared at me with piercing green eyes. Her red hair gleamed like a new coin in the sunlight and her hoop earrings swung as she moved. 'Yes, sonny?'

I knew how a popped balloon must feel. If I weren't such a shrimp, she wouldn't have used that word. Drawing myself up to my full height, I said, 'Ms Brown, Dad wants you to prune your bougainvillea. You see, he's entering the garden competition and –'

'Sure,' she said. 'No problem. Right away.'

From our dining room which overlooked her yard, I heard the noise of a motor revving. It sounded like a chainsaw. Rushing to the window, I saw Elvira with both hands poised above her head like an executioner before making a swooping motion with the device and neatly lopping the bougainvillea canes along with the head of Dad's topiary bird.

Dad flipped his lid when he saw the carnage. Forgetting to be intimidated as he always was with women, he confronted Elvira in her backyard. His angry words poured out in a rush. 'You imbecile, that was a work of art you just destroyed.' He was unintelligible and woefully embarrassing.

Elvira's eyebrows formed twin peaks of surprise as she tried to get a word in edgewise. 'I'm really very sorry. It was an accident. Perhaps we can talk this out.'

Dad was all hot air and bluster so the only response he could manage was a strangled grunt before he retreated to the house.

Late in the afternoon, he pruned his hedge to a flattened shape and life resumed its normal pattern, with Dad gardening and me just hanging about. My mates lived over the other side of town so, bored and restless, I had to entertain myself.

There was only a fortnight to the competition and Dad was on edge.

Our nights were disturbed by Mabel's caterwauling on the back fence and yowling and fighting of her prospective suitors. It didn't help when a cat scratched in Dad's pansy bed and left mangled flowers lying on the path.

Dad decided to complain to the council. It always made my skin prickle when he did that. My mates and I didn't dob. He was well-known down there and I could just imagine their irritation.

He was told, 'It's nothing a well-aimed boot won't cure. And, after all, we've had several unfounded complaints from you about another neighbour and isn't there such a thing as crying wolf? However, we'll pass it on.'

In the following days when Dad was out, Elvira and I chatted over the back fence. The day before the garden competition, I asked her to do a tarot reading for me.

In her kitchen, she laid out three cards and turning one over she said, 'Your father doesn't like me. I can see trouble ahead for him. Don't be like your father. Too much emotion causes people to act irrationally and makes enemies.'

The council must have contacted her.

'And the future?'

'Not what your father expects, sonny.'

This was not good news for Dad. The garden competition must be down the drain.

Turning to her shelves of herbal remedies, I asked in what I hoped was a manly tone, 'Do you have a potion for stunted growth?' But my voice broke in the middle and spoilt the effect.

She picked up a phial and said, 'This is reputed to be useful.' She looked me up and down and added, 'Your dad would never approve.'

She turned away and I slipped the bottle in my pocket. As I was leaving, I thought I saw some garden gnomes in an adjoining room.

There were no instructions on Elvira's bottle, so I took a quick swallow before falling asleep. I awoke to a chanting noise. Was it in my head or was it coming from outside?

Feeling slightly dizzy, I struggled to the window. The garden was lit by a full moon. Unbelieving, I rubbed my eyes. Prancing round and round the flowering plum were six garden gnomes.

I went to wake Dad but his only response was, 'You're having a nightmare, son.'

By the time I returned to the window, the moon had gone behind a cloud and in the shadows I could see the gnomes lying in a heap under the tree.

They were still lying there in the morning covered with withered flowering plum blossoms with a path of singed grass encircling the tree.

Dad didn't win the competition. He had trouble explaining the presence of the gnomes and the judges said his lawn was tacky. He blamed jealous rival competitors but I had my own ideas.

Running the Gauntlet

On a midwinter's day in a country town, when welfare payments weren't covering their extravagant habits, Harry and Tom decided to enter the dodgy profession of cattle duffing.

They'd abandoned break and enter a week before when they were breathalysed on their way to a job. During a routine inspection of the vehicle, the constable found their tools of trade, and while he couldn't pin anything on them, he warned them he'd be keeping a close eye on their activities in the future.

The cattle duffing idea came to them, or rather to Tom – Harry was slow-witted – in a local bar when they were partaking of a counter lunch. Seated beside them was local identity Bob Farley and a fellow grazier they didn't know.

Bob Farley was holding forth on the subject of his livestock. 'My Angus bull was grand champion at the last show. It was the talk of the town. I was offered ten thousand dollars for him but I knocked it back. A good bull's worth his weight in gold.'

Tom cast a glance at Harry, but he was gnawing on a chop bone and oblivious to the significance of this piece of information. Tom jabbed him in the ribs, and related to him sotto voce what he had just heard, and added, 'I know a mate who'd give a couple of thousand smackers under the lap for that bull. I'll give him a call.'

'You're kiddin'. We don't know nothin' about bulls.'

'An Angus bull,' said Tom, 'that's those black ones, you idiot. That's all we need to know. Besides,' he continued, puffing out his skinny chest. 'I've had stock experience. Three months at the piggery.'

He had only lasted a short while because the owner took a dim view of the way his animals were treated. The pigs, too, had objected to being manhandled and took every opportunity that presented itself to bite any part of his anatomy that came within range.

Smarting from the slur on his astuteness and eager to contribute to the coming operation, Harry said, 'I can lay me hands on a horse trailer and we can use the old Toyota ute.'

Whenever they trundled down the highway in the ute, smoke billowed from the exhaust. It wasn't registered, but they had to make do. The burglary trade had not been lucrative.

Tom and Harry studied the situation for several weeks. The Farley property was a couple of kilometres off the main highway and down a quiet gravel road.

'How will we get in?' asked Harry, scratching his head.

'No problem.' said Tom. 'We'll come well-prepared. With a cattle prod, some rope, some hay as a bribe and bolt-cutters for the lock. We'll go in when there's a full moon.'

Harry's vacuous blue eyes shone with admiration. 'Geez, Tom. You've thought of everything.'

So, on a moonlit night with the horse trailer in tow, they arrived at the Farleys' gate, tense and jittery, in spite of the coolness of the evening. While Tom was dealing with a lock and chain, Harry, impatient because it was taking too long, decided to scale the barbed wire fence. He put one foot on the middle wire and cocked his other leg across only to be hooked by the crutch of his pants.

'Tom,' he bleated. 'I'm stuck.'

Muttering, Tom yanked Harry free and tore off the patch of denim left behind on the wire. 'We don't want to leave evidence.'

Spooked by the shadows cast by the moonlight, Harry lifted his feet up high and put them gently but noisily down on the frosted ground.

'No need for that,' said Tom. 'The cows are up the hill watching us. That must be the bull. The one like a ten-ton truck.' He turned to spread the hay.

The cows, anticipating a feed, came careering down the slope with the bull well out in front. He tried to stop, but skidded on the icy turf and, with all his legs stiff like pieces of four-by-four, he shot past the trailer and an astonished Tom and Harry. The cows, more sedate, ambled up, calling their calves.

'Crikey,' was all the normally voluble Tom could manage.

The bull, having overstepped his target through no fault of his own, hastily returned.

Tom observed, 'He has a ring in his nose. That's handy. You can pull him along with the rope while I use the cattle prod.'

Harry slipped the rope through the bull's nose. That was the easy part. The bull, however, wasn't cooperative. He objected to being shifted from his unexpected treasure as well as the electric shock to his rump, so he started snorting and pawing the ground.

'Look out,' shouted Tom. 'He's going to charge.'

Harry's reactions were always slow. He stared in stupefaction at the animal a moment too long before being shot like a stone from a catapult into the air and landing with a thump in the horse float.

Forestalling any criticism of his methods, Tom said, 'I told you to run. Don't you ever listen? You always were a nitwit.'

They decided to try a different tack. The remnants of the hay were spread from the bull into the trailer. The bull steadily munched his way up the ramp and into the back. While the two men were performing high fives and congratulating themselves on their cleverness, the bull started to back out. They locked the tailboard hastily and drove out down the road.

The trailer swayed ominously as the bull slid from side to side and back and forth his hooves clattering on the wooden floor.

'Take it easy, Tom. We got a lot of kilometres to the farmer's place.'

Just as they were a short distance down the road, there was a loud bang like a giant firecracker and the truck and trailer slewed into a ditch. As the vehicle shuddered to a halt, there was the sound of splintering wood.

Harry said in awe, 'The tyre's blown and the bull's gone through the bottom of the trailer.'

Harry's stating of the obvious always irritated Tom and he snapped, 'You don't have to be Einstein to know that. Get out and have a look.'

They discovered the bull had indeed gone through the floor of the trailer. While Harry was scratching and bleating, Tom took command.

'Get the axe. We'll cut him free.'

Harry hacked the floor planks and the now frantic bull found it could back out. Ignoring the two men, it bolted, darting across the road, weaving through the bushes. Their last view of it was a black mass knocking down saplings in its mad dash to freedom.

Harry croaked, 'That was a fizzer.'

Tom, who couldn't think of a way to blame Harry, snapped, 'Put the tools in the bag. The truck and trailer aren't registered. They'll never trace it. We'll head for the coast. You never know what we'll find down there.'

So they trudged off to the highway leaving behind the truck and trailer, fingerprints and Harry's wallet.

Killing Two Birds

'Down from thar hills, Sarah Mae.'

My name is Sarah. Irene adds the Mae so she's sure we all get the point. That's the third time she's called me a hillbilly. I tuck my scuffed shoes under the seat.

There's a circle of us year 10 girls under the wattle tree in the playground of our high school. It's home time. Irene is the leader of the group and the others all edge towards her. I blink my eyes to hide the tears. My hopes of being one of the group scuttled.

'Crybaby,' jeers Jillian.

I stand up and tug hard at my uniform to straighten it over my knees as I move off. My hand clasps the patch on the side. It reminds me of Irene's taunt.

I hear footsteps pounding along the pavement after me. It's Irene.

'I'll race you up the street, Sarah Mae.'

I decline. If you beat Irene at anything, it puts her in a foul mood. I know because I've beaten her heaps of times. When I scored a higher mark today in maths, she turned and looked at me. Her eyes struck me like the chill of frost on bare feet.

She fixes me with those cold grey eyes now. I feel trapped as if under guard and my instinct is to give her the slip.

'Want to do me a favour?' she asks. 'Then I'll owe you one.'

'Depends,' I hedge, weighing up what the benefits might be, if any. Did I really want to be part of the inner sanctum?

'OK.' I mutter.

'I'm going to old Lady Muck's house to do some cleaning. You can help.'

Mrs Jones, that's her proper name, lives alone in a cul-de-sac a short walk from school. Irene had made a rude gesture when Mrs Jones reprimanded her at the shopping centre for smoking. I'm surprised that she has agreed to help her.

We pass a garden ablaze with colour. Irene calmly rips the heads off several agapanthus, trampling along the pansy border and laughs.

'What did you do that for?' I ask hot with embarrassment. I decide Irene is an idiot and turn to walk away.

'Give me your wallet,' she says.

'What are you going to do now?' I ask, half fascinated, half repelled under the spell of those chill grey eyes.

'Watch me,' she says and drags my silver coin along the side of a parked car. The screech of the coin on metal sets my teeth on edge.

She races off up the road like a shot when I tell her there's someone coming. There isn't. But I can't resist trying to take the mickey out of her. I move along so I won't be held responsible.

There's no sign of anybody at Mrs Jones'. I walk up the path with its trellis of climbing roses and tap at the open door.

Irene yanks me in. 'She's shopping. The key was under the mat. I saw her put it there.'

I look around. 'It's a beautiful house.'

Irene licks her lips. It reminds me of a dog savouring a succulent bone.

There's a sound of running water down the hall.

'Turn off the tap, Irene. You'll have a flood.'

'Can't find the key.'

She disappears humming down the hall. I hear the sound of drawers being turned out and I follow her in.

'You've really done it,' I say with awe.

She slits the down pillows with a flourish worthy of the local butcher. Clouds of feathers flutter as silent as snowflakes and settle on her hair and shoulders. Irene shrieks and leaps around intoxicated with a primitive war dance of rage and release.

I pad back over the flooded carpet. Singing and laughing, Irene dances behind me into the lounge. She heads for the sideboard. Her arm swoops across the surface like the wing of a giant bird and sends the china crashing and tinkling to the floor.

I leave the house too stunned to talk.

'I still owe you one,' shouts Irene.

The wind whips my hair as I step into the sun. I don't notice at first the group passing by. They are Irene's friends. There is nothing friendly in their faces.

At seven that night, I sit at my desk doing homework. I can't believe what Irene had done. There is no question of being her friend. Or the friend of any of her friends. I become aware of my mother shouting up the stairs. It makes me uneasy. Mum never disturbs my homework. Clutching the banister, I pad down the wooden treads. My mother is twisting her hands anxiously at the front door. Two policemen loom in the door frame.

'We want a word with you, young lady. There was an incident this afternoon at 28 Gregory Place. Your wallet was found on the premises and you were seen leaving. You'd better come down to the station.'

Clara

Clara stood watching him as he sat on the log he had just felled and saw the dejection on his face as he fingered his lower lip. 'What is it, Fred?' she asked tremulously.

The sun slipped behind a cloud and the scrub felt dank and chill as with an involuntary movement she grasped the child tighter to her chest. In the clearing, the cabin with its iron roof was starting to cool. The north wind which had blown all day had dropped. She often came into the scrub with her husband to escape the heat of the cabin and its iron roof.

'Thompson's plough's buggered. He was goin' to help with the scrub and sowing. Can't do it on my own and we can't afford to hire men. I'll go down Ballarat way to get work.'

'Will you be gone long?' She scuffed her feet in the fallen leaves and bit her lip drawing blood.

'Can't say. You'll be right. I'll leave Blue and the rifle. Don't go blubberin' on me, girl,' he said, the anger in his voice making her cringe.

She was a town girl born and bred and she shivered at the notion of the long days alone which stretched out before her. Her fear went deeper than mere loneliness. What if Tom should come looking for her? She'd never mentioned him to Fred. That was not an association she was proud of. Gentle and slight of figure, she was not built to withstand the rigours of the bush. Mustering the sheep with her husband had roughened the texture of the skin on her face and hands. There was only one horse and Fred would need it. The nearest township was two miles along the track that passed through the clearing in front of the house. She thought of asking to go with him. But Fred liked the company of his mates and didn't want to be hogtied to a sheila. There were few passers-by, mostly men on horseback stopping to ask for a drink. There was the occasional swagman demanding beer and cursing her when she said there was none.

One had called three days after her husband had gone. She looked forward to the news these passers-by brought if they were civil. She'd been rounding up the sheep with Blue to pen them for the night. The sun's rays dipped in the west and the trees that edged the clearing cast long shadows. A family of kangaroos stood like sentinels among the gum trees before hopping away silently back into the scrub.

Blue growled a low guttural warning as the man approached. Her scalp prickled with a shock of recognition.

His eyes looked from her face to her feet and back again. 'Still have a fine figger, Clara.'

She felt a chill of fear as with an involuntary movement she grasped the dog's collar.

'They told me in town you were on your own. I've been looking all over for you, girl. Didn't take kindly to you running out on me.'

'It was over, Tom. You can't stay. I don't want any trouble. I'll get you some tucker, then leave.'

The cawing of crows overhead reminded her of her solitude.

He waved his hand in a mock salute as he stood aside to let her enter the cabin. After she brought him bread and tea, he sat on the tree trunk her husband had felled and wolfed it down.

When she closed the shutters, he called out, 'You don't have to be afraid of me –' but he broke off and muttered into his beard. This made her even more nervous.

She bolted the door and the dog settled on the hearth as she prepared baby for bed. But Blue got up and kept pacing back and forth near the door and whimpering and it set her teeth on edge. Through a crack in the door she saw his silhouette against the fading light hunched facing the shanty. She sat on a chair at the kitchen table with the rifle across her knees prepared for a long vigil. Her husband, although careless of most matters concerning her welfare, had taught her to shoot. It was past midnight and the only sounds she could hear were the steady ticking of the clock and the thudding of her heart against her ribs. The candle had gone out and the only light was the glow from the fire. Knowing Tom was still out there had stretched her nerves to breaking point. There was an insistent knocking at the door. The voice was hard and violent.

'Jest need a blanket, Clara.'

Fearful he'd hear the trembling in her voice, she didn't answer. He would take pleasure in her fear. She poked at the dying embers and put on fresh logs from the stack beside the hearth. The baby slept fitfully in the corner and she needed to be brave for him. When she was dozing in the chair, the sound of feet scrunching in the leaves made her instantly alert. The fire had made the room hot and its flames threw shadows on the walls of the cabin increasing her unease. The hands holding the rifle were shaking. She'd moved to the door when she heard his footsteps but she felt her legs giving way and she staggered and there was silence. Although she was straining her ears for sounds, the thud of rocks on the roof was unexpected and made her call out in fear. He had always known how to frighten her and would keep on until she begged for mercy. That was his way. She put down the rifle to pick up the baby and peered through the crack in the door. The moon's rays shone in the clearing but Tom was out of sight.

There were scuffling noises at the back of the cabin. At first, she couldn't place them. He was piling up leaves. Then she thought she heard a match strike. The crackling sounds were unmistakable. Wisps of smoke drifted through the cracks of the cabin. It stung her throat. The significance of his actions hit home. He was trying to smoke her out and she and her child would be at his mercy. Putting her baby back in his cot, she picked up the gun and unfastened the bolt of the door. The smoke billowed out and she stepped over the threshold as flames started to lick at the slabs of the back wall. Tom came round the side of the cabin. The sight of the gun aimed at him startled him.

'Put the gun down, Clara. What do you know about guns?' he sneered. 'You was always skeered stiff of 'em.'

'You've left me no choice, Tom. This time you've gone too far.'

He kept coming, seemingly confident of his power over her. She slammed the bolt home and pulled the trigger. Falling backwards, he landed with a thud. The bullet had penetrated his left side and blood started seeping onto his shirt. Darting into the blazing cabin, she brought baby to safety babbling incoherently. After she laid baby on the grass, she picked up the shovel and started to dig frantically at the back of the gutted cabin. Light streaked the eastern sky as she laid down the shovel and dragged Tom's body to the grave. She was too distraught to notice that there was still breath in him. A magpie chorus filled the clearing with an outpouring of joyous song but she was deaf to its beauty and only conscious of the task at hand. Covering the body with clods of earth, she gathered leaves to hide the bare ground. She crossed herself not out of any reverential feeling but out of superstitious fear.

Shortly after, two policeman rode up.

One said, 'Are you hurt, missus? Where's your husband? We'll send a buggy to take you and the little 'un back to town. By the by, bin any strangers this way lately? Settlers in the district have been robbed.'

They had their minds on other matters and were oblivious to the way she was wringing her hands.

They cantered back into the scrub and she rose to her feet and trod wearily to the back of the still smouldering cabin. The grave was empty and the earth and leaves flung aside. She grabbed the shovel and started to dig and as she dug deeper, her frantic whimperings turned to mad shrieks for she saw his shadow on the ground beside her and knew he would show no mercy.

The Cyclone Ghost

The night of the cyclone changed our lives forever.

Rain was lashing the windows with a fury and the wailing wind made me think of banshees. The gas lamp in the centre of the table yellowed the room and when we moved our shadows moved in unison like ghostly puppets.

Dad and I were playing chess. You can't do much else in a blackout. But we weren't talking because the rain was pounding on the iron roof like hammer blows and the sound was deafening. The roof leaked and Dad had set the frying pan under the drip but the steady plop of water was a distraction.

I was letting Dad win. He never smiled these days. I moved my rook away when I had him in a checkmate position and he didn't even notice how generous I was. Lately, whenever Mum travelled on council business, he became gloomy. She didn't leave us to our own devices. All we had to do was heat the meals she left in the freezer. I always thought it was a woman's role to nag but that's all Dad seemed to do these days.

Before Mum left for the station, they had a big barney.

'You're dedicated to two things,' Dad ranted. 'That useless dog out there and being a councillor.'

'My job helps keep the wolf from the door,' Mum said and as a parting shot, 'Be on time tomorrow night.'

Dad's shoulders sagged. The sugar cane farm was all he'd known. His father died when he was thirteen. He'd had to grow up quickly and had been running the farm by himself ever since. 'It's the man's role to be the breadwinner,' he'd drummed into me. 'You can take over in a few years.' But I'd other ideas I'd confided to Mum.

Like her, most of the wives had off-farm incomes. Dad couldn't accept that.

When I looked at him in the lamplight, I saw myself in thirty years if I stayed – the same grizzled hair, furrowed forehead and weather-beaten look from years in a tropical sun. His face looked chiselled in the dim light. I sensed disappointment in the droop of his mouth and I felt sorry for him.

He must have sensed my pity. His black mood started to lift and he became what Mum called maudlin. He aired thoughts he'd never told me before. 'I wanted to get educated too. Like your mother. Then I could have been the councillor. Junketing around. Having fun.'

So he was jealous of Mum. I shifted uneasily on my chair thinking of the local school fete. The one Mum opened. I was on the veranda looking in. She was inside with another councillor. Their heads were close and I thought they were looking deep into each other's eyes like they do in the movies.

A man came along the veranda and called out, 'Hey! What are you doing?'

I ducked my head and moved away.

I could hear Mum's dog Rufus, a red setter, bark. He was chained to his kennel near the house. I walked over to the window and rubbed a space in the mist. Rain was running down the window pane in rivulets. It was impossible to make out much in the pitch dark. Just shapes. The branch of the poinciana was banging against the shed but Rufus had stopped barking.

'Can't I bring him inside, Dad? Mum always has him in when it rains.'

'Well, she's not here. Don't see why we should take over her chores. Leave him there.'

Spite. That's what it sounded like.

The clock struck nine.

'Time to pick her up at the station,' Dad said.

We put on our oilskins and Dad backed out the truck. Rufus had started howling, an eerie sound as he never howled. Just barked. Dad swore under his breath as he crashed the gears. The cane cyclone was flattening the cane and that meant the year's income gone, so I could share his frustration.

Dad put the truck in four-wheel drive but it still slewed in the mud.

'The phone lines must be down or Mum would have rung,' I said placatingly.

The road to the station was through sugar cane flats and across a river which flowed down from the ranges behind.

We didn't speak and the only sounds in the cabin were the monotonous thud of the windscreen wipers and the splash of water as the truck cut a swath through the pools on the road. Like our farm, the fierce wind was flattening the cane on either side.

'We'll be in trouble if the engine cuts out,' said Dad grimly.

We were nearing the river crossing when the lights revealed a shape moving out of the bushes and across in front of the truck.

'Watch out, Dad.' I peered into the gleam of the headlights. 'It's Rufus.'

Dad jammed his foot on the brake and yanked at the wheel as the truck spun into a ditch.

I climbed out to fetch Rufus. But he was nowhere to be seen. I turned when I heard the roar of the river and the sound of cracking timber as a huge wave washed away the bridge.

Dad and I drove home in silence. We rushed over to Rufus's kennel. He was lying leashed outside in the rain and didn't stir as we approached.

Dad bent to examine him and said quietly, 'He's dead, son.'

When Mum was able to come home a fortnight later, Dad left it to me to explain as best I could what had happened.

She was glad we were safe but shed tears over Rufus.

The vet said he had a heart attack. After a while, Dad brought home a red setter puppy.

Dynamo

The antics of the Spears' dog, Dynamo, kept the whole district supplied with a constant source of complaint. And its hapless owners too, for that matter.

'A sheep dog who doesn't recognise a sheep but rounds up the chickens instead,' said Ted Spear, shaking his head in disgust as he watched his wife from the safety of the veranda.

'Get out of that pen, you useless creature,' shouted Mary Spear with her nightgown flapping around her skinny ankles, swatting at Dynamo with the straw broom, feathers and dust mingling in the air as she carried out a morning ritual. Her pullets weren't laying and she'd have to fill in the hole Dynamo had dug under the hen run again.

'Get Ronald to give you a hand, Hon,' called Ted Spear helpfully.

But their son Ronald was nowhere to be seen and Mary muttered something that could have been 'That layabout' as she pushed Dynamo out the hole. With his tail upright like a flag of defiance and his mouth stretched from ear to ear, if dogs can smile then Dynamo was grinning.

But the bush telegraph was humming overtime and Dynamo the chief topic of conversation. Marauding dogs led by a big, red, lop-eared mongrel were killing sheep and the word was out that it was Dynamo.

Ted decided it was time to move to town. He couldn't handle the sheep without a good, working dog. Ronald could find a job. There was no question of getting rid of Dynamo. He was Ronald's dog and it would break his heart if he had to part with him. Ronald had found Dynamo through an advertisement in the local paper. 'Working Dog Parents. Free to a good home.' This appealed to Mary's deeply embedded frugality and Ted, well, Ted always went along with what Mary wanted anyway. It saved arguing, and talking meant unnecessary effort.

When Ronald's bovine, brown eyes focused on Dynamo's lustrous yellow ones, a bond was forged. Their young neighbour who had been bitten by Dynamo retrieving his tennis ball called them 'fellow ferals'.

Mary, suspicious of a relationship she didn't understand, told her friends, 'That dog's hypnotised him. I'm sure of it.'

But it was more the case of a strong character influencing a weak one.

But complaints about Dynamo soon surfaced when they settled in town. A collector for a respectable charity was the first to voice her displeasure. It was Mary who had to deal with the matter. At such times, Ted and Ronald always made themselves scarce.

She answered the doorbell to find an hysterical, red-faced lady with Dynamo's jaws firmly clamped around her arm.

Mary took the offensive. 'We don't take unsolicited callers here,' she said in a loud voice. 'Besides, you're invading the dog's territory.' Mary was not in the habit of defending Dynamo but she felt the occasion warranted it.

'You should put a beware of the dog sign on your gate, madam.'

Dynamo had let go the collector's arm and was alternately growling and sniffing her shoes.

'He's only escorting you to the door.'

'And what if he decides his mouthful will make a succulent bone?'

The next one with a justifiable grievance was the man who read the meter for the electricity company. When Ronald came home from job-hunting, the poor fellow was bailed up against the house by a truculent Dynamo barking furiously.

His relief at seeing Ronald overshadowed his anger at half a workday wasted. 'I've been here all afternoon, mate. He let me in all right but he bloomin' well wouldn't let me out.'

Ronald as always was able to put a positive spin on Dynamo's peccadilloes. 'No burglar will get near the place, Mum,' he said, puffing out his chest with pride and slipping his chop bones to Dynamo under the cover of the dinner table as a reward.

Because of Ronald's attachment to the dog, Mary's disapproval didn't extend beyond keeping a column marked Dynamo in her household expenses book. Ronald could contribute when he found a job or maybe, if she reached the end of her tether, it could be used as evidence that Dynamo had to go.

There was the time Dynamo chewed a large piece out of the TV cabinet. It was still on Ted's list of things to be done around the house. Mary, who prided herself on keeping a spick and span home, felt it was the focus of all eyes when visitors came. Dynamo had a fondness for chewing her shrubs, especially the camellias, and even devoured some rose bushes. Heaven knows how he swallowed the prickles.

There was the irritation of Dynamo on Mary's favourite sofa at night with his head on Ronald's lap at one end and his tail wagging under her nose at the other. When her doctor asked what irritants were in their house to upset her asthma, she said one word: 'Dynamo'.

High on her list of household expenses was a pair of Sheridan sheets. She still recalled with horror the time Dynamo used the clothesline on washday as a canine merry-go-round. Washday was her favourite day of the week. She loved the thrill of wet washing flapping on the line, the heavenly scent of Omo, the delectable pink of her Sheridan sheets, and so apparently did Dynamo. She came outside after a quick nap to find the wind spinning the clothesline out of control and Dynamo hanging on for dear life to her now shredded sheets.

One of Ronald's chores was to take his dog for a walk each day. But with all Dynamo's pent-up energy, it was more like a gallop around the neighbourhood as he strained on the leash and dragged Ronald along. Ronald, who was not given to exertion, soon tired of this and let Dynamo out for solo romps.

Mary's first intimation of trouble in the air came with a knock at the door from the police.

'We've had a complaint, madam, about a big, red, savage dog. He chased a cyclist in the local shopping centre and bit him on the leg tearing his trousers. Could I see your animal?'

Mary thought it certainly sounded like Dynamo. She fetched him on a rope but Dynamo, agitated at seeing an intruder on his territory, promptly bit him on the hand.

The sergeant, remarkably restrained, took the rope and said, 'He'll have to come along with me.' But he was unprepared for the strength of Dynamo, who with a mighty jerk freed himself and tore off down the road.

Ted and a very disconsolate Ronald scoured the streets for days with unaccustomed perseverance to no avail. Dynamo never reappeared.

Mary didn't let on but she went direct to the police station to make enquiries and considered the matter closed when she read the police noticeboard under 'Persons of Interest' – 'Wanted. A large red dog named Dynamo. Approach with caution. Savage and dangerous.'

The Spears now have a cat called Fluffy.

A Matter of Taste

Carly is twenty-five and not yet married and the thought is like a gnat flitting about in my mother's head. She is a widow and owns a business in the shopping mall called A Quilting Bee and hopes to retire to the coast soon. My mother wants to get her settled before she leaves. All my mother's friends have married daughters. Her friends come to afternoon tea and discuss future grandchildren.

'Carly is doing well at university,' my mother says proudly but her voice trails off and her friends look embarrassed and bring out their knitting. They understand her concerns and are sympathetic.

'She doesn't even date,' she complains to me later in the kitchen when I'm reading the newspaper and she's preparing a cup of tea.

I shuffle the pages and heave a sigh.

My mother feels it's a matter for a sister to broach. 'Have a word with her.'

I bring up the subject that night when she comes out of the shower in her chenille dressing gown and tartan slippers and a towel turban-style around her head.

'What about dating again?' I say. It's not an easy subject for her to talk about. She was stood up twice and is afraid it could happen again.

'No way. I end up doing younger sister's assignments while they date my friends from uni.'

She blinks at me and I know that is something that will never change.

Her glasses slide down her nose. Characteristically, she pushes them up. 'You know what they say about men and glasses,' she says.

'Join a chat room, for heaven's sake. Then you can be what you want to be.'

My mother is very dubious about it. 'In my day, we went dancing,' she grumbles.

'At least she'll have social interaction of a sort,' I say.

Privately, I think she's not cut out for a chat room. She finds it hard to dissemble. I warn her, 'For many people, it's just pretence.'

Carly is unsure about it. She never played make-believe as a child so it doesn't appeal. Her favourite toy was an abacus. She decides to give it a week.

It's very hard to get her to take the plunge. She was like that with swimming lessons. A toe in the water to test the temperature, a shudder and a grimace and a hasty retreat to the change cubicles. My mother spent a fortune on unused lessons. Finally, when she was going through the ritual for the umpteenth time, I pushed her in and off she went.

Carly reads up on statistics on marriage. She is studying to be an actuary and statistics is an area that she knows a lot about. More and more people are remaining single but married people tend to live longer and she considers these thoughts for quite a while.

She gets very nervy as the time she has allocated to start approaches and snaps at my mother when she asks her if she wants a cup of cocoa and her favourite – fish paste on toast.

On Sunday night, she logs on to the Internet and joins a chat room as Lily. She gives us strict instructions that no one is allowed to interrupt and the TV must be turned down. She comes out after ninety minutes with a little smile at the corner of her mouth. That is a good sign. Carly never smiles if things are going badly. She gives it the thumbs-up sign but decides to change her name to something less old-fashioned as two sixty-year-olds had asked for her phone number and one wanted to take her old-time dancing.

I really think my mother has made Carly too comfortable at home and she will only make a move when our mother sells up. We encourage her to persevere.

Carly is a whiz at figures but can't spot a fraud. She seeks my advice on possible choices. She has a list of contacts that would last her for a month of Sundays. I peruse it carefully and then rule out Brad Pitt look-alikes. Even if that is not gross exaggeration, Carly is no Jennifer Aniston. The four who claim they own a Porsche I dismiss as 'If only...' types. One plays the stock exchange for a living.

'Gambling is not one of my interests,' she says priggishly.

I hide a smile and fail to point out that joining a chat room with a view to dating could be seen as a gamble.

Carly really enters into the spirit of this pursuit of happiness and takes to titivating in front of the mirror. We decide it would be an idea if she makes a list of what she considers are desirable attributes in these would-be dates.

'A perfect match would be studying at university,' she says. 'There's been a dearth of those on the Internet so far. It's probably too frivolous a pastime.' She ponders this matter for several minutes.

I bring her back to the matter at hand before she's sidetracked into analysing the pros and cons of pastimes.

'An interest in politics would be a bonus,' she decides. 'We could have in-depth discussions about the state of the world.' Carly rarely watches TV because she is so busy and seldom opens a newspaper, so this is just twaddle.

'Tall and dark and –' She catches my eye and gives a silly grin.

She is a hopeless romantic but I have to bring her back to earth. 'That's the stuff of Mills and Boon.'

She settles for an unemployed Arts graduate who plays chess in his spare time and keeps guinea pigs. Carly asks if she can bring him home for their first date. Apparently, that was Frederick's choice of venue. He arrives promptly at seven with, to our surprise, his mother.

'What shall we call you?' I ask him politely. 'Fred or Ricky?'

'We prefer Frederick,' says his mother, who continues to manage the conversation for the rest of the night, sitting quite at home between Carly and Frederick. It is not easy to figure out what Frederick thinks of this. His eyes are hidden behind tortoiseshell glasses with thick lenses.

For the next few weeks, there is no further mention of Frederick. There is a discreet acknowledgment that the date was not a success. My mother says not to bring up the subject in front of Carly as it might embarrass her.

Carly gives up preening in front of the mirror and reverts to wearing her uni gear, sweatshirt and jeans.

My mother's chilblains are causing her problems, so I take over the cooking and Carly manages the shopping on Saturdays.

It's Saturday afternoon. There's the sound of footsteps and the rustle of plastic bags in the hall.

Carly comes in pink with excitement followed by a tall, presentable young man. She speaks and the words tumble over each other as she puts down her bags. 'This is Geoffrey. We met at the supermarket. He's a plumber and he loves fish paste on toast.'

Brunhilda's Revenge

Brunhilda Brown, daughter of a German migrant, was frightened of black snakes, tarantulas and things that howl in the night. Her father had left her in his will a small grape-growing property on the Central Tablelands. To her dismay, her neighbours, the Martyns, coveted her property and as several members of the clan had been incarcerated from time to time for varied offences such as cattle-duffing, passing bad cheques, loitering and impersonating a police officer, she was apprehensive.

All Brunhilda wanted was peace and quiet in her own little haven. Being rather fond of glühwein and other German treats, her waistline had vanished and, with a generous bosom into the bargain, she had never been popular with the local striplings. She kept herself to herself and lived alone.

The postman called every morning promptly at ten and at the sound of his horn Brunhilda always bustled out to the gate. There could be a letter from her grandmother in Munich or a cheque for her last consignment of grapes. Instead, there was a small brown-paper-wrapped parcel. Filled with curiosity, Brunhilda fumbled with the paper and lifted the lid off a box.

She stood rooted to the spot and turned as green as her grapes in the vineyard as she gazed at the reality of her worst nightmare – a tarantula. Her nerveless fingers dropped the box and the hairy creature scuttled away under a geranium plant.

It took an hour for her body to stop quivering and she took some deep breaths to settle her nerves. What was she going to do? She knew who the culprits were. The Martyns of course.

A phone call to the local constabulary had little effect. 'There's no proof of sender.'

That night, she was just settling cosily in front of the fire when she heard footsteps outside and the staccato of rocks on the roof. She sat frozen in her chair and her heart started thumping at an alarming rate. The silence that followed was punctuated only by the ticking of the clock. She twitched a curtain aside and thought she saw moving shadows.

Her mind moved in slow motion. She had an aversion to guns but surely now was the time to get her father's old shotgun. Loading it shakily, she flung open her front door and fired. There was a wild yell, retreating footsteps and swear words Brunhilda had never heard before. She closed her door and went to bed.

The visit from a constable the next morning was not unexpected.

'We've had a complaint, Miss Brown.'

'Oh yes?' said Brunhilda.

'A man who is known to us was shot. He's in a doctor's surgery having pellets removed from a delicate part of his anatomy.'

Brunhilda felt an adrenalin rush of satisfaction. 'I was out shooting rabbits,' she volunteered, 'but I didn't see anyone.'

'We won't be pursuing our inquiries any further. He was obviously trespassing. By the by, there are some large rocks on your roof. Keep your door locked at night. You never know what's afoot.'

Ornamental Cabbage

It would have been a perfect morning had I not noticed the neighbour's lawn chair sitting on my bed of ornamental cabbage. My neighbour is a biggish woman about the size of Cassius Clay so, as might be expected, I am rather intimidated by her.

But nevertheless I asked her what I thought was an ordinary question for an extraordinary situation. 'Why is your lawn chair in my bed of ornamental cabbage?'

'I threw it there. My slug of a husband spends all his time sitting in his lawn chair. If he wants his chair, he can fetch it. And if he fetches it, he can't come back.'

The next day, I opened my window to a less than perfect morning when I noticed my neighbour's husband sitting in the lawn chair in my bed of ornamental cabbage and frolicking at his feet was their great Dane.

So I asked my neighbour's wife, 'Why is your great Dane in my bed of ornamental cabbage?'

'I put him there. He's my husband's pet. He bit the postman, who's going to sue.'

For no reason my husband could discern, we moved house. We no longer grow ornamental cabbage.

CPSIA information can be obtained
at www.ICGtesting.com
Printed in the USA
LVHW110926100822
725537LV00004B/208